DRUGS

MARIJUANA
A MyReportLinks.com Book

Michelle Laliberte

MyReportLinks.com Books
an imprint of

Enslow Publishers, Inc. E
Box 398, 40 Industrial Road
Berkeley Heights, NJ 07922
USA

MyReportLinks.com Books, an imprint of Enslow Publishers, Inc. MyReportLinks®
is a registered trademark of Enslow Publishers, Inc.

Library of Congress Cataloging-in-Publication Data

Laliberte, Michelle.
  Marijuana / Michelle Laliberte.
     p. cm. — (Drugs)
  Includes bibliographical references and index.
  ISBN 0-7660-5281-8
  1. Marijuana—Juvenile literature. 2. Marijuana abuse—Juvenile literature. I. Title. II. Drugs (Berkeley
Heights, N.J.)
  QP801.C27L34 2005
  362.29'5—dc22
                                 2004008176

Printed in the United States of America

10 9 8 7 6 5 4 3 2

To Our Readers:
Through the purchase of this book, you and your library gain access to the Report Links that specifically back
up this book.
The Publisher will provide access to the Report Links that back up this book and will keep these Report Links
up to date on **www.myreportlinks.com** for five years from the book's first publication date.
We have done our best to make sure all Internet addresses in this book were active and appropriate when we went
to press. However, the author and the Publisher have no control over, and assume no liability for, the material
available on those Internet sites or on other Web sites they may link to.
The usage of the MyReportLinks.com Books Web site is subject to the terms and conditions stated on the Usage
Policy Statement on **www.myreportlinks.com**.
A password may be required to access the Report Links that back up this book. The password is found on the
bottom of page 4 of this book.
Any comments or suggestions can be sent by e-mail to comments@myreportlinks.com or to the address on the
back cover.

Photo Credits: Clipart.com, p. 3 (cannabis); © 2004 Partnership for a Drug-Free America, p. 36; Girl Power!,
p. 23; Hemera Photo Objects, pp. 1, 14; Library of Congress, p. 18; MyReportLinks.com Books, p. 4; National
Archives, pp. 28, 30; Photos.com, p. 35; Stockbyte Sensitive Issues, pp. 15, 25, 26; U.S. Department of Health
and Human Services, pp. 12, 19; U.S. Drug Enforcement Administration, pp. 3 (bong and loose leaves), 9, 10,
21, 32, 39, 41.

Cover Photo: Hemera Photo Objects (main photo); National Archives (photo on top bar).

Disclaimer: While the stories of abuse in this book are real, many of the names have been changed.

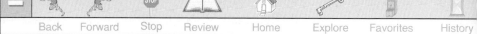
About MyReportLinks.com Books

MyReportLinks.com Books
Great Books, Great Links, Great for Research!

The Internet sites listed on the next four pages can save you hours of research time. These Internet sites—we call them "Report Links"—are constantly changing, but we keep them up to date on our Web site.

Give it a try! Type http://www.myreportlinks.com into your browser, click on the series title, then the book title, and scroll down to the Report Links listed for this book.

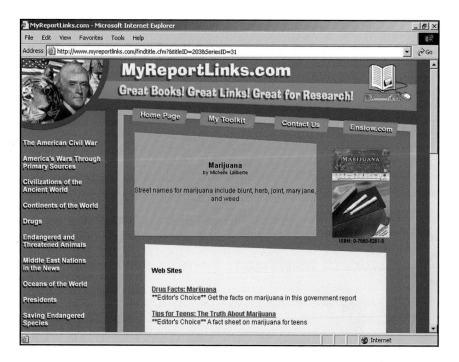

The Report Links will bring you to great source documents, photographs, and illustrations. MyReportLinks.com Books save you time, feature Report Links that are kept up to date, and make report writing easier than ever!

Please see "To Our Readers" on the copyright page for important information about this book, the MyReportLinks.com Web site, and the Report Links that back up this book.

Please enter **DRW2673** if asked for a password.

Report Links

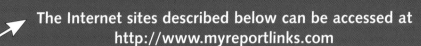

The Internet sites described below can be accessed at
http://www.myreportlinks.com

▶**Drug Facts: Marijuana**   *EDITOR'S CHOICE

This Web site provides information on the extent of marijuana use and its
effects on health, treatment, arrests, production, trafficking, and legislation.

▶**Tips for Teens: The Truth About Marijuana**   *EDITOR'S CHOICE

The information available at this Web site clears up some myths
concerning marijuana and helps to give a clear picture of the effects, signs,
and risks of using this drug.

▶**Marijuana**   *EDITOR'S CHOICE

THC is the active ingredient in marijuana, and research shows that it
interferes with the normal functioning of many areas of the brain. This
article discusses the effects of marijuana on the central nervous system,
including the brain.

▶**The Brain's Response to Marijuana**   *EDITOR'S CHOICE

Learn what marijuana can do to your brain and nervous system. Read
about your body's reaction to the presence of THC. Follow the links at
the bottom of the pages to read more.

▶**NIDA InfoFacts: Marijuana**   *EDITOR'S CHOICE

Information is provided on the extent of marijuana use and its effects on
the brain, heart, lungs, pregnancy, and learning. Read about the drug's
addiction potential and treatment problems.

                                              *EDITOR'S CHOICE

▶**Busted: America's War on Marijuana**

This Web site contains a lot of information on marijuana. View a
historical time line of marijuana use, and read interviews with some of
America's drug experts, as well as overviews of D.A.R.E., case histories,
laws, sentencing, and prices. Take the marijuana quiz.

Report Links

The Internet sites described below can be accessed at
http://www.myreportlinks.com

▶ **Body FX**

Did you ever wonder what marijuana does to your brain and lungs? The drug also adversely effects the body's immune system. Learn more from the Girl Power! Web site about marijuana and what it can do to you.

▶ **Cognitive Deficits in Marijuana Smokers Persist**

New research suggests that the effects of smoking marijuana continue long after use, with impairments to a person's thinking skills lasting at least twenty-eight days. Learn more about this research on this site from the National Institute on Drug Abuse.

▶ **Did "Sixties' Parents" Use Hurt their Kids?**

If your parents smoked marijuana, are you more likely to? The answer is yes. Teens with parents who use or have used marijuana were three times as likely to have used the drug when compared to teens whose parents have never tried it. Read more about this connection at this Web site.

▶ **Drug Abuse: Marijuana**

On this Web site from PBS, you will find basic information on marijuana, including signs of use, health risks, and other consequences. Try the drug abuse crossword puzzle. There is also a Spanish version.

▶ **Exposing the Myth of Smoked Medical Marijuana**

Does marijuana pose health risks to users? Does marijuana have any medical value? This government Web site answers these and other important questions concerning medical marijuana.

▶ **Facts on Drugs: Marijuana**

This NIDA for Teens Web site answers questions about marijuana, including how many teens are using the drug and what it can do to you. Follow the links on the left-hand side and at the top for more information. Take the marijuana quiz to test your knowledge.

▶ **Freevibe.com: Marijuana**

On the FreeVibe Web site, you will learn what you need to know about marijuana. Take the marijuana knowledge test, and read the tips for saying "no" to marijuana, as well as personal stories written by teenagers.

▶ **Initiation of Marijuana Use: Trends, Patterns, and Implications**

You will find a large number of statistics, graphs, and charts on marijuana use from this Web site. Information on use by state, age, gender, and race is available. Read the section on early marijuana use and later drug use patterns to learn more about marijuana as a gateway drug.

Any comments? Contact us: **comments@myreportlinks.com**

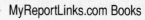
Report Links

The Internet sites described below can be accessed at http://www.myreportlinks.com

▶Marijuana Abuse

Using marijuana can cause adverse physical, mental, emotional, and behavioral changes to your body. Read more about marijuana and what it can do to you.

▶Marijuana and Teens: Fact Sheet

Teenagers mistakenly think that marijuana is a safe drug to use. From the Office of National Drug Control Policy Web site, read about marijuana's risks to your health and its affects on academic achievement and behavior.

▶Marijuana Anonymous

Based on the Alcoholics Anonymous Twelve Step program, MA helps people addicted to marijuana. A variety of literature is offered on the site free of charge. The association also provides online meetings.

▶Marijuana Use in Supportive Care for Cancer Patients

Marijuana is sometimes used to help cancer patients with nausea, vomiting, and loss of appetite caused by chemotherapy. Learn more from this article from the National Cancer Institute.

▶Marijuana: Facts for Teens

At this National Institute on Drug Abuse Web site you will learn what marijuana and hashish can do to your brain and body, including the harm to unborn fetuses. Short- and long-term effects are noted. Information is also provided on the drug's connection with traffic accidents.

▶NAADAC, The Association for Addiction Professionals

NAADAC focuses on drug, tobacco, alcohol, and gaming addictions in an effort to create healthier families and communities through prevention, intervention, and quality treatment. Learn more about this organization at their Web site.

▶Narcotics Anonymous

Based on a twelve-step program, Narcotics Anonymous works to help those addicted to drugs recover from their addiction. NA can be found in over one hundred countries. Follow the links to find worldwide contact and meeting information. Bulletins, reports, and periodicals are also available.

▶ONDCP Fact Sheet: Marijuana

Information is provided on marijuana's background, effects, extent of use, and consequences. Facts about availability, law enforcement, and statistics on treatment are also included.

Report Links

The Internet sites described below can be accessed at
http://www.myreportlinks.com

▶**Partnership for a Drug-Free America**

Partnership for a Drug-Free America focuses its efforts on reducing substance abuse in the United States. You will find a recent study on teen drug use, an e-newsletter you can sign up for, and stories of real people.

▶**Street Terms: Marijuana**

You will find an extensive collection of terms used by drug dealers and users to describe marijuana and the activities surrounding its use. This is a valuable resource for parents, teachers, and students.

▶**Study Demonstrates that Marijuana Smokers Experience Significant Withdrawal**

A research study has found that people who stop smoking marijuana suffer withdrawal symptoms, some as severe as those associated with tobacco smoking. Symptoms can include headaches, restlessness, depression, and irritability.

▶**Substance Abuse Treatment Facility Locator**

Updated annually, this Web site includes both private and public substance abuse treatment facilities. These programs are approved by either the governments of individual states, the Department of Veterans Affairs, the Indian Health Service, and/or the Department of Defense.

▶**U.S. Drug Enforcement Administration: Marijuana**

Follow the link for "What Americans Need to Know about Marijuana" to read the myths of marijuana use. You will also learn the medical, social, and economic consequences of using this drug. Lots of important information is available at this Web site.

▶**Weeding Out the Genetics of Marijuana Use**

A study examined the relationship between marijuana use and genetics as well as the relationship between marijuana use and later use of harder drugs. Read a brief overview of this study and its results at this Web site.

▶**What You Need to Know About Drugs: Marijuana**

This fact sheet explains what marijuana is and what it is sometimes called. It also provides information on how marijuana is used and how it affects the body.

▶**What's Up With Marijuana?**

This site from the Drug Enforcement Administration provides an informative page on marijuana. Learn where it comes from, what it looks like, the effects of using it, and more.

MARIJUANA FACTS

✗ Marijuana is the most widely used illicit drug in the United States.

✗ Marijuana is the third most popular recreational drug of choice. (Alcohol and nicotine are the top two.)

✗ According to a 2001 survey, 20 percent of eighth graders tried marijuana at least once, and by tenth grade, 20 percent were current users.

✗ In 2002, about 697,000 of a total of 1,538,813 million drug arrests in America were for marijuana offenses. That is 45.3 percent of all offenses.

✗ Users spent $10.6 billion on marijuana in 1999.

✗ Marijuana enforcement alone costs American taxpayers between $7.5 and $10 billion annually.

✗ Marijuana tends to be the first illicit drug that teens use.

✗ Nearly one in ten teens aged twelve to seventeen currently uses marijuana in the United States.

✗ In 2000, over 3 million youths aged twelve to seventeen used marijuana at least once.

✗ A marijuana smoker is arrested every forty-five seconds in America.

✗ In 2002, 283,527 people entered drug abuse treatment programs and reported that marijuana was their main drug of abuse.

✗ The government spends an average of $15.7 billion annually on efforts toward the war on illegal drugs, including marijuana.

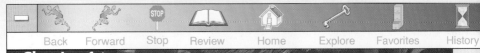
WHAT IS MARIJUANA?

Marijuana, a green, brown, or gray mixture of dried leaves, stems, seeds, and flowers of the hemp plant, *Cannabis sativa,* is the most commonly used illicit drug in the United States.[1] According to a 2001 National Household Survey on Drug Abuse, more than 83 million Americans aged twelve and older have tried marijuana.[2]

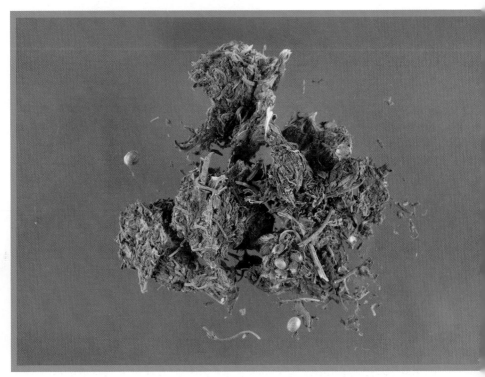

▲ Marijuana is often sold as a green, leafy substance. The leaves come from the hemp plant, known scientifically as Cannabis sativa. That is why marijuana is sometimes called cannabis.

Cannabis and hemp are terms for marijuana and other drugs made from the same plant. Northern Lights and Colombian are just two of the many types of marijuana grown around the world. Marijuana is known to users by many other slang names such as pot, grass, herb, Mary Jane, weed, and reefer.

Strong forms of cannabis include sinsemilla, hashish, and hash oil. Sinsemilla is made from just the buds and flowering tops of female plants. Hashish is the sticky resin from the female plant's flowers, and hash oil is a tar-like liquid distilled from hashish.

Scope of Marijuana Use With Adolescents

Marijuana use is widespread among adolescents and young adults. During the 2001 Monitoring the Future survey, students from the eighth, tenth, and twelfth grades were asked about their marijuana use. Twenty percent of eighth graders said they had tried using marijuana at least once, and by tenth grade, 20 percent were steady users. Among twelfth graders, nearly 50 percent had tried marijuana or hash at least once, and 20 percent were current users.[3]

Children and young teens start using marijuana for many reasons. Some are simply "just curious" while others feel they need to "fit in" at all costs. One former marijuana user, seventeen-year-old Mackenzie, learned the hard way what kinds of problems are caused by mixing curiosity with drugs.

Mackenzie's Personal Struggle*

"I mostly started out of curiosity, but never to fit in," Mackenzie said. "I never thought of myself as someone who would smoke pot. In fact, I used to be one of those people who looked down on those who did."

Mackenzie realized in her freshman year of high school that, to her peers, smoking pot was not the big deal it had been in

*Disclaimer: While the stories of abuse in this book are real, many of the names have been changed.

junior high. The kids were not afraid of using it or being caught with it. In fact, it was widely accepted as the drug of choice at teen social gatherings. So the first time the opportunity presented itself at a party, Mackenzie "burned," or "smoked up," with a few friends.

"Nothing happened, which only led to a deeper curiosity," admits Mackenzie. "I continued to try until I was convinced that I couldn't get high. I was just about to stop trying, but then it happened." After an afternoon of driving around with friends and smoking pot, Mackenzie achieved the intoxicating feeling, or "high," that marijuana creates in users.

"I felt so relaxed and so happy all at the same time," Mackenzie recalls. "I just wanted paper and pencil so I could

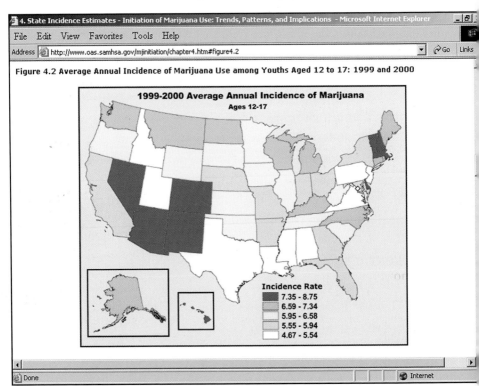

In the year spanning 1999 to 2000, new marijuana use among twelve to seventeen year olds was most widespread in the states shaded the darkest. Those states with the least amount of new marijuana use are in white.

draw everything around me. Music was the most amazing of it all. It was like all my emotions put to music."

This is when Mackenzie's use of marijuana increased.

"I began to smoke more and more. I was smoking every weekend and occasionally on the weekdays too."

The Wrong Crowd

Mackenzie soon became friends with people who burn, or smoke, which led to more daily intake of pot. Soon she started buying her own bags and her own drug paraphernalia, such as pipes. Then she began to use a "one-hit" or a "one-hitter," which is a smoking device that looks like a hollowed-out cigarette and holds a "hit" of marijuana. This made it too convenient to sneak tokes of pot all the time.

"I found myself doing a lot of sneaking and coming home high. I was eating packs of gum and going through bottles of body spray and eye drops in a week. I just felt deceitful and like I was a bad person."

Even though Mackenzie felt this way, she still continued to smoke pot. Her caution to hide her drug use started slipping as she noticed how clueless her parents were to her drug use.

"I started driving around with it and just became less and less careful," Mackenzie said.

One night, Mackenzie sat in her car waiting for a girlfriend. Her friend was in a nearby car arguing with her boyfriend. They did not know that the police were observing their behavior. To the cops, the scene fit the description of a typical drug deal in progress. As a result of her carelessness, Mackenzie got arrested for possession of drug paraphernalia, but no drugs were found in her possession. Mackenzie is now considered a juvenile delinquent and awaits a court date for fining and sentencing. At a minimum, Mackenzie will be required to attend a twenty-one-hour intensive boot-camp-style drug awareness program at the county jail. If she had been caught with the drug on her person, the punishment could have been much worse.

Mackenzie has given up her use of marijuana and is currently dealing with the problems her drug use has caused her. She believes getting into trouble really helped her.

"No matter how great you may think it is, it is still illegal. It took getting busted to open my eyes to that fact. I was never dependent upon it. It was just an escape. Life is hard, and sometimes people find different ways to help themselves through it."

Mackenzie found new ways of staying away from drugs. She kept herself busy by focusing on life's positives, like her school work and job, plus Mackenzie surrounded herself with a different group of friends who did not get "high."

How Is Marijuana Used?

Most marijuana users roll loose marijuana into a cigarette called a joint, or smoke it in a pipe or water pipe called a bong. Another popular method for some users involves slicing open a cigar and replacing the tobacco with marijuana, making what is called a blunt. Some users mix marijuana into foods or use it to brew a tea.

All forms of cannabis are mind-altering or psychoactive drugs. They all contain THC (delta-9-tetrahydrocannabinol), the major active chemical in marijuana that causes the mind-altering effects of marijuana intoxication.

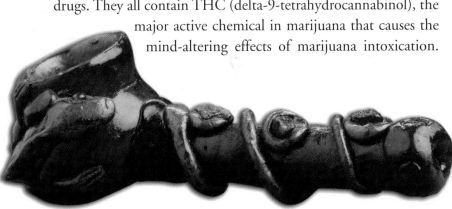

▲ Clay pipes are just one of the many devices that people use to smoke, or inhale, marijuana.

Perhaps the most common way to inhale marijuana is through smoking a joint, such as the one this man appears to be rolling.

Forms of cannabis also contain more than four hundred other harmful chemicals.[4]

Marijuana's effects on the user depend on the strength or potency of the THC it contains. The drug enters the brain immediately upon smoking marijuana, causing the user to feel euphoric or "high." This feeling can last anywhere from one to three hours. Smoking marijuana deposits several times more THC into the blood than does eating or drinking the drug.[5]

For the year 2001, based on marijuana confiscated by law enforcement agencies, most ordinary marijuana contains an average of 5 percent THC.[6] Sinsemilla and hashish, or hash, contain 9 percent THC. Hash oil contains an average of 19 percent THC.[7] THC potency of marijuana has increased since the 1970s and continues to increase.[8]

HISTORY OF MARIJUANA

Marijuana use can be traced back to China around 6000 B.C.[1] The Chinese used cannabis seeds for food. Hemp seeds have been used as a food source for their nutritional value. Seeds can be ground to make flour, pressed for the oil, or toasted as a snack. Today some hemp enthusiasts are developing new products containing hemp, like granola bars and ice cream. Hemp seeds are also used to make birdseed. The seeds are sterilized so as not to contain any THC. Bird fanciers even claim parakeets will not sing unless fed hemp seeds.[2]

Hemp is the world's strongest natural fiber and has been used to make cloth and rope for more than ten thousand years. Hemp cloth and ropes are durable, more mildew resistant, and cheaper to produce than cloth made from cotton. Hemp can be used to make anything currently made from cotton, timber, or petroleum. George Washington and Thomas Jefferson both grew hemp. Benjamin Franklin owned a mill that made hemp paper. Thomas Jefferson wrote the Declaration of Independence on hemp paper. Until 1883, more than 75 percent of the world's paper was made with hemp fiber. A 1937 issue of *Popular Science* magazine named hemp "The New Billion Dollar Crop." Industrial hemp contains less than one percent of THC, the psychoactive component of marijuana.[3]

Marijuana was used for its medicinal values as early as five thousand years ago.[4] Western medicine welcomed marijuana's medical benefits in the mid-1800s. By the early twentieth century, more than one hundred papers had been published by physicians recommending it to treat a variety of illnesses.

Marijuana's Social History in America

In the United States between 1850 and 1937, marijuana was widely used as a drug and could easily be bought in pharmacies and general stores. Yet recreational use of marijuana remained limited until the 1920s and 1930s, when it became recognized as an intoxicant.[5] An intoxicant is a substance that impairs a person's physical or mental control. The recreational use of marijuana

STREET TERMS FOR MARIJUANA USE	
TERM	DEFINITION
420	Marijuana use
BC bud	High-grade marijuana from Canada
Blunt	Cigar filled with marijuana
Bong	Device used to smoke marijuana
Bud	Marijuana
Chronic	Marijuana
Dope	Marijuana
Ganja	Marijuana from Jamaica
Grass	Marijuana
Herb	Marijuana
Homegrown	Marijuana grown by the user
Hydro	Marijuana grown in water
Indo	Marijuana from Northern California
Joint	Marijuana cigarette
Kind bud	High-quality marijuana
Mary Jane	Marijuana
One hit	Device for inhaling a small amount of marijuana
Pot	Marijuana
Reefer	Marijuana
Shake	Marijuana
Sinsemilla	Potent marijuana
Weed	Marijuana

Source: Office of National Drug Control Policy

became mostly associated with Mexican-American immigrant workers and the African-American jazz musician community. It was during this time that hemp a person can ingest was renamed "marihuana" and the plant's long-lived history as a cash crop was replaced with a new image: "The Devil's Weed."[6]

In 1930, the Federal Bureau of Narcotics (FBN), founded by the federal government, was headed up by Commissioner Harry Anslinger. Also at this time, Dupont Chemical Corporation started developing new synthetic materials. These new materials included nylon and specifically rayon. Hemp had been primarily used as the fiber for making rope and clothes at the time. Hemp was cheaper and stronger. Rayon would have been unable to compete with the strength of hemp or its economical manufacturing process.

A 1930s campaign led by Anslinger sought to portray marijuana as a powerful, addicting substance that would lead users into narcotics addiction. This is why marijuana has also been called "The Gateway Drug."[7] In addition, during the Great Depression, Mexican workers in border towns were using marijuana. All sorts of lurid stories appeared in newspapers connecting violent crimes committed by Mexicans to marijuana use. Soon all minorities

Harry Anslinger was once the commissioner of the Federal Bureau of Narcotics. He was responsible for leading the movement to ban hemp in the United States.

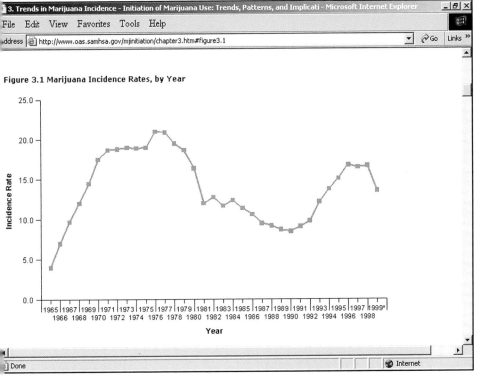

Figure 3.1 Marijuana Incidence Rates, by Year

New marijuana use increased significantly in the 1960s and early 1970s. It peaked in 1976 and 1977. New use decreased throughout the 1980s only to increase again in the early 1990s. This peaked in 1996 and decreased for the rest of the decade.

were placed under a microscope, and marijuana was viewed as the connecting factor.[8]

In 1937, Congress passed the Marijuana Tax Act, which made cannabis illegal in the United States. Although the bill was not specifically aimed at hemp production, legal limitations put an end to the prominent hemp industry. Stricter sentencing laws from 1951 to 1956 set mandatory minimum jail sentences for drug-related crime.[9] However, recreational marijuana use began to spread into middle-class white America in the 1960s. As a symbol of rebellion against authority, college students of the sixties and "hippies" also used marijuana.

▷ The Marijuana Epidemic and the Controversy

Marijuana use by mainstream white Americans began increasing. The government responded by passing the Comprehensive Drug Abuse Prevention and Control Act of 1970. Congress ended mandatory penalties for drug offenses for marijuana. Marijuana was also categorized separately from other narcotics, and the National Organization for the Reform of Marijuana Laws (NORML) was born that same year.[10] NORML's mission is to legalize marijuana use so that the use of cannabis by adults will no longer be a crime. NORML also supports the medicinal use of marijuana as well as the industrial uses of hemp.

In the late 1970s, President Jimmy Carter, his administration, and his drug policy assistant, Dr. Peter Bourne, sought to make marijuana use less of a crime. The president, himself, asked Congress to abolish federal criminal penalties for anyone caught with less than an ounce of marijuana.[11] But a grass-roots parents' movement lobbied for stricter regulations and was responsible in changing public opinion.

The Anti-Drug Abuse Act, signed by President Ronald Reagan in 1986, reinstated previous mandatory minimums and raised federal penalties for drug possession and distribution.

According to a 1999 United Nations report, 141 million people around the world used marijuana at that time. This represented 2.5 percent of the world population.[12] It is the most commonly used illicit drug and the third most popular drug of choice in America. Currently more Americans use marijuana than either cocaine or heroin. Yet studies show that the younger a person is the first time he or she uses marijuana, the more likely he or she is to use cocaine or heroin in the future.[13]

Marijuana use is widespread among adolescents and young adults. Research indicates that nearly 50 percent of teenagers try marijuana before they graduate from high school.[14] After a decade of decreasing use, marijuana smoking began an upward trend once more in the early 1990s, especially among teenagers.[15] By

Marinol is a prescription drug composed of man-made THC. The drug has been found to relieve chemotherapy patients of nausea and vomiting, as well as help AIDS patients regain their appetite.

the end of the decade though, this upswing had leveled off well below former peaks of use.

Debate Over Marijuana and its Medicinal Value

The first recorded use of cannabis as medicine was a Chinese medical compendium in 2737 B.C.[16] In the *United States Pharmacopoeia*, marijuana was listed from 1850 to 1942.[17]

It was used to treat lack of appetite, gout, migraines, pain, hysteria, depression, rheumatism, and many other illnesses.[18]

After 1937, it was illegal to grow, possess, or distribute marijuana. This made it difficult for the medical community to prescribe medicinal marijuana to suffering patients. Then the Compassionate Use Program of 1975 was established by the U.S. Food & Drug Administration, which allowed doctors to prescribe marijuana to their patients for medical use.

The Anti-Drug Abuse Act of 1986 reinstated mandatory minimums and raised federal penalties for possession and distribution. Between 1978 and 1996, legislatures in thirty-four states passed laws recognizing marijuana's therapeutic value for people suffering from painful diseases. Twenty-five of these laws remain in effect today.[19]

However, in 1996 California enacted Proposition 215, which legalized medical marijuana use for people suffering from AIDS, cancer, and other serious illnesses. A similar bill was passed in Arizona that same year. Ten states have passed medical marijuana laws since 1996: Alaska, Arizona, California, Colorado, Hawaii, Maine, Maryland, Nevada, Oregon, and Washington.[20]

Is THC Safe?

THC, the main ingredient in marijuana, produces effects that potentially can be useful for treating a variety of medical conditions.[21] It is the main ingredient in an oral medication that is currently used to treat nausea in cancer chemotherapy patients and to stimulate appetite in patients with AIDS.[22]

However, the inconsistent levels of THC in different marijuana plants pose a major hindrance to research and to the safe and effective use of the drug. These differing dosages of THC cause the strength and duration of effectiveness to vary. Plus, ingesting marijuana does not produce results for hours and often produces different results in different patients.

Adverse side effects of marijuana smoke on the respiratory system can offset the helpfulness of smoking the drug for some patients. In addition, little is known about the many other chemicals besides THC that are in marijuana that could have detrimental effects on patients with other medical conditions.

Chapter 3 ▶

MARIJUANA'S EFFECTS ON THE BODY

Marijuana affects many areas of a user's system. The potency of the THC in marijuana determines the effects on the body. When someone smokes marijuana, THC rapidly passes from the lungs into the bloodstream, which carries the chemical to all the major organs throughout the body. THC is stored in the fat cells of the body, brain, liver, and kidneys. Marijuana can

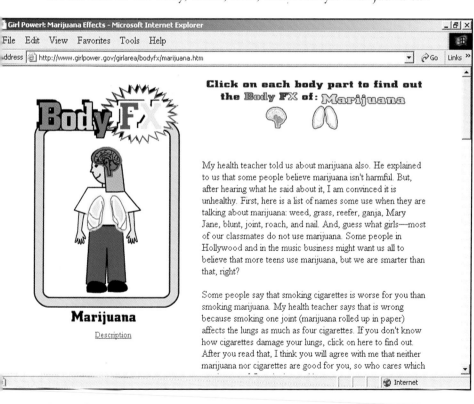

Girl Power! Marijuana Effects - Microsoft Internet Explorer   _ | 8 | ×

File   Edit   View   Favorites   Tools   Help

ddress http://www.girlpower.gov/girlarea/bodyfx/marijuana.htm   Go   Links »

Click on each body part to find out the Body FX of: Marijuana

Body FX

Marijuana

Description

My health teacher told us about marijuana also. He explained to us that some people believe marijuana isn't harmful. But, after hearing what he said about it, I am convinced it is unhealthy. First, here is a list of names some use when they are talking about marijuana: weed, grass, reefer, ganja, Mary Jane, blunt, joint, roach, and nail. And, guess what girls—most of our classmates do not use marijuana. Some people in Hollywood and in the music business might want us all to believe that more teens use marijuana, but we are smarter than that, right?

Some people say that smoking cigarettes is worse for you than smoking marijuana. My health teacher says that is wrong because smoking one joint (marijuana rolled up in paper) affects the lungs as much as four cigarettes. If you don't know how cigarettes damage your lungs, click on here to find out. After you read that, I think you will agree with me that neither marijuana nor cigarettes are good for you, so who cares which

Internet

▲ Three of the major parts of your body affected by marijuana are your brain, lungs, and immune system.

remain in the system from ten to thirty days depending on how much is smoked and how often.[1]

Short-term Effects on the Body

Within minutes of inhaling marijuana smoke, a user's heart begins beating rapidly and the bronchial passages relax and become enlarged. Blood vessels in the eyes expand, making the eyes look red. A marijuana user may experience pleasant sensations, and colors and sounds may seem more intense. Time appears to pass very slowly. The user becomes very thirsty as his or her mouth becomes dry, a term often referred to as "cotton mouth." The user suddenly becomes very hungry. A user's hands may grow cold and tremble. After the euphoria passes, he or she may feel sleepy or depressed. Sometimes marijuana use causes anxiety, panic attacks, or paranoia and distrust.

Effects on the Brain

Marijuana's effects begin immediately after the drug enters the brain. Effects can last from one to three hours. As the THC enters the brain, it causes a user to feel "euphoric" or "high" by acting in the brain's reward system. THC activates the reward system in the same way nearly all drugs of abuse do. They stimulate the brain cells to release the chemical dopamine.

In the brain, THC connects to specific sites called cannabinoid receptors on nerve cells and thereby can influence the activity of those cells. Some areas of the brain have many cannabinoid receptors, while other parts have few or none. Many cannabinoid receptors are found in the parts of the brain that influence pleasure, memory, thought, concentration, sensory and time perception, and coordinated movement.[2]

Effects on the Lungs

People who smoke marijuana regularly may develop many of the same breathing problems that tobacco smokers have. These

▲ *Research has shown that smoking marijuana may cause even more damage to a person's lungs than smoking tobacco cigarettes.*

include daily cough and phlegm problems, more frequent chest colds, and a heightened risk of lung infections. Cancer of the respiratory tract and lungs may also be promoted by marijuana smoke. Marijuana smoke contains 50 to 70 percent more carcinogenic (cancer-causing) hydrocarbons than tobacco smoke.[3]

It also produces an enzyme that converts certain hydrocarbons into their cancer-causing forms, which may accelerate changes that produce malignant cells.

▷ Long-term Health Effects

Long-term marijuana use can lead to addiction for some people. It is both emotionally and mentally addictive.[4] Marijuana addiction is classified as compulsive, often characterized by uncontrollable marijuana craving, seeking, and use, even when the user knows it is not in his or her best interest. Users will find they need increased amounts of marijuana to achieve intoxication. This is referred to as "chasing the first high," and it is never attainable. Along with the craving, physical withdrawal symptoms can make it hard for long-term marijuana smokers to stop using the drug. People trying to quit have reported irritability, difficulty sleeping, and anxiety. They also display increased aggression on psychological tests, peaking approximately one week after they last used the drug.

Increased and long-term use of marijuana can lead to risk of chronic coughs, bronchitis, and emphysema. A study comparing 173 cancer patients and 176 healthy individuals produced strong evidence that smoking marijuana increases the likelihood of developing cancer of the neck or head.[5] Let us not forget that marijuana also has the potential of promoting lung cancer because it contains irritants and carcinogens.

Chronic marijuana smoking has been found to weaken a user's immune system. Your immune system is needed to protect your body from harmful things. In a weakened immune system, your body loses the ability to stop allergies, pollens, bacteria, or viruses from making the body sick.[6]

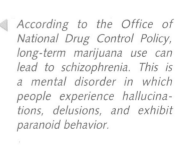

According to the Office of National Drug Control Policy, long-term marijuana use can lead to schizophrenia. This is a mental disorder in which people experience hallucinations, delusions, and exhibit paranoid behavior.

Chapter 4 ▶

HOW MARIJUANA IS CULTIVATED AND SOLD

It is estimated that marijuana consumers in the United States spent $11 billion in 1998 and $9 billion in 1990 on marijuana.[1] The worldwide production of marijuana is a big business. According to the Bureau of International Narcotics Matters at the U.S. Department of State, it is estimated that in 1991, 26,052 tons of marijuana was produced worldwide.[2]

Cultivation and Distribution of Marijuana

From 1850 to 1937, marijuana was easy to buy in pharmacies and general stores because it was legal. Recreational use of the drug was not popular until shortly after the Mexican Revolution of 1910, which brought an influx of Mexican immigrants introducing the habit.

The Volstead Act of 1920 made drinking alcohol illegal. People began to see marijuana as an attractive alternative to the high cost of getting illegal alcohol. The act raised the price of alcohol in the United States, which ultimately led to an increase in use of marijuana. Signs were hung in jazz clubs selling marijuana for 25 cents or less. By the 1930s, there were reportedly more than five hundred of these "tea pads" in New York alone. As unemployment rose during the Great Depression, so did resentment of the Mexican immigrants who were taking jobs and their connection to marijuana use. Numerous research studies conducted showed marijuana use by lower-class communities who had crime and violence. So by 1937, Congress passed the Marijuana Tax Act, which made it a crime to sell or possess the

This is how the cannabis plant looks as it is growing.

drug. The increased use of marijuana in the 1960s led to the Comprehensive Drug Abuse Prevention and Control Act of 1970. This act adopted a broad definition of a "drug dependent person" to make it easier to provide treatment for both addicts and other individuals with other drug abuse problems. It allowed scientific and medical determinations relative to scheduling of controlled substances. Soon mandatory penalties for drug offenses were abolished by Congress, and marijuana was categorized separately from other narcotics.

The Controlled Substances Act of 1970, placed all substances regulated under federal law into five schedules based on the substance's medical use. Marijuana was classified along with heroin and LSD as a Schedule I drug. This defined as a drug that has the highest abuse potential and no accepted medical use.[3]

Most marijuana came from Mexico at that time. The Mexican government agreed in 1975 to destroy the crop by spraying it with a toxic herbicide called paraquat.[4] After that, Colombia became the main supplier. However, due to the huge profit and lower bulk of cocaine, Colombia no longer leads in marijuana supply. Currently, Mexico is once again chief among the countries making marijuana available in the United States.

Getting Tough on Drugs

The Reagan and George H. W. Bush administrations (in office from 1981 to 1993) pushed for the passage of stricter laws and a heightened vigilance at the southern borders. In addition, mandatory sentences for possession of marijuana were passed. As a result, the "war on drugs" shifted from reliance on imported marijuana to domestic cultivation, particularly in California and Hawaii.[5]

Then, beginning in 1982, the Drug Enforcement Agency turned increased attention to marijuana farms in the United States. There was a shift to the indoor hydroponic growing of plants specially developed for small size but high yield.[6]

▲ *Marijuana distributors often sell the drug to dealers in bricks. The dealers break it into small amounts to sell. This brick has been confiscated by law enforcement authorities.*

Since hydroponic operations do not require soil, marijuana can be rooted in porous material such as lava rock or rock wool. Using state-of-the-art delivery systems for water, fertilizers, carbon dioxide, and light, the sophisticated indoor growing techniques of marijuana suppliers can produce marijuana superior to that which is grown outdoors. Further, the indoor marijuana plant can come to maturity and be harvested within a four-month cycle, thus yielding a potential for three harvests a year.

Marijuana Prices

During the early 1980s, prices for commercial-grade marijuana varied from $350 to $600 a pound.[7] In the first six months of 1996, the price for a pound of marijuana ranged from $200 to $4,000, averaging about $800 per pound.[8] Sinsemilla, whose female plants yield a much higher THC content, ranged in cost from $1,000 to $2,000 per pound.[9]

Prices per pound varied considerably depending on a marijuana consumer's distance from the Mexican border. In the Southwest, Mexican marijuana sells from $400 to $1,000 per pound.[10] In the Midwest and Northeast, prices increase and range from $700 to $2,000 per pound.[11] Profit margins increase significantly as marijuana is sold to United States consumers further from the Southwest border. For example, 500 pounds of marijuana

MARIJUANA USE BY ARRESTEES, 2003		
PAST USE	**MALES**	**FEMALES**
In last 7 days	39.3%	30.0%
In last 30 days	44.9%	36.0%
In last year	51.9%	44.4%
Average # of days used in last month	10.5 days	9.1 days

Source: Arrestee Drug Abuse Monitoring Program

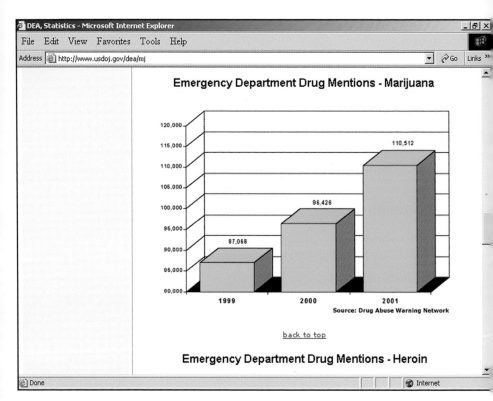

Emergency Department Drug Mentions - Marijuana

110,512

96,426

87,068

1999   2000   2001

Source: Drug Abuse Warning Network

back to top

Emergency Department Drug Mentions - Heroin

The number of times marijuana was mentioned in emergency room incidents increased by 23,444 over the period of 1999 through 2001.

bought in Mexico for $50,000 can be sold in St. Louis, Missouri, for $400,000.[12]

Dangers of Using Drugs

Drugs are related to crime in many ways. It is a crime to use, possess, manufacture, or distribute drugs classified as having abuse potential. Severity of the penalty varies based on the amount of marijuana found in one's possession. Penalties also vary depending on if a person is selling or growing marijuana or where he or she grows or sells it. Lengthy jail terms can be imposed to those who sell marijuana near schools. Marijuana laws vary from state to state, but carrying marijuana is illegal in all fifty states.

Users have caused auto accidents while under the influence of marijuana. Using the drug can affect many skills required for safe driving. Marijuana can make it hard to judge distances and react to sounds, road signals, and traffic. Its use can also lead to the loss of one's driver's license, loss of an occupational license, and loss of child custody. Under state and federal forfeiture laws, many suspected marijuana offenders lose their cars, cash, boats, land, business equipment, and houses.[13] Eighty percent of the individuals whose assets are seized are never charged with a crime.[14] Drugs are not worth the risks.

Effects on American Society

The government spends an average of $15.7 billion annually on the war on drugs.[15] In addition, state and local governments spend $16 billion more per year to enforce drug laws.[16] The number of marijuana-related arrests is staggering. In 1995, nearly 600,000 of a total of 1.5 million drug arrests in America were for marijuana offenses.[17] Marijuana enforcement alone costs American taxpayers between $7.5 and $10 billion annually.[18]

A 1997 study reported that law enforcement authorities arrested a marijuana smoker every forty-five seconds in America.[19] In 2002, 45.3 percent of the 1,538,813 total drug abuse arrests were for marijuana.[20] Of those 697,082 marijuana arrests, 613,986 were arrested for marijuana possession alone.[21]

Chapter 5 ▶

Avoiding Marijuana and Getting Help

Children and young teens start using marijuana for many reasons. Research has shown that students who smoke marijuana are generally less successful than their peers.

The use of alcohol and drugs by other family members plays a significant role in whether young people start using drugs. If parents, grandparents, or older brothers and sisters abuse drugs, it sends the wrong message to the young people who follow them and see them as role models. Some children who take drugs do not get along with their parents.

Less than half of all teenagers say they have tried marijuana but say "it's easier to buy than cigarettes or beer," according to a national survey.[1] More than one third of teens polled by the National Center on Addiction and Substance Abuse said they could buy marijuana in just a few hours, 27 percent in an hour or less.[2]

All aspects of a child's environment—home, school, and neighborhood—help to influence whether he or she will try drugs. Some children are exposed to a network of friends or peers who pressure them to use. Others mention psychological coping as a reason for use; it helps to deal with anxiety, anger, depression, boredom, and so on. Marijuana use is not an effective method for coping with life's problems. Staying "high" can be a way of avoiding the problems and challenges of growing up.

▶ Signs of Marijuana Use

Marijuana users exhibit physical signs of use. If someone is "high" on marijuana, they might:

- Seem dizzy and have trouble walking
- Act silly and giggly for no reason
- Have very red, bloodshot eyes
- Have a hard time remembering things that just happened
- Become very sleepy after the effects fade

Other physical signs to look for are:

- Evidence of drugs or drug paraphernalia, including pipes, bongs, or rolling papers
- Odors on clothes or in bedroom
- Use of incense and other deodorizers

▲ Sometimes people that children meet at school will influence them negatively. However, if a user is caught with marijuana or other drugs at school the penalties are more severe.

- Use eye drops or excessive colognes or perfumes
- Display posters, clothes, or jewelry promoting drug use

Other Reasons to Avoid Marijuana

Long-term marijuana use creates an altered perception of reality, including hallucinations, delusions, and suspicious thoughts in chronic users. Because of these effects, users could be involved in auto crashes.

Marijuana also affects many other motor skills required for safe driving such as alertness, the ability to concentrate, coordination, and reaction times. Marijuana use can make it hard to judge distances and react to signals and sounds on the road.

▲ Marijuana is often referred to as a gateway drug. This means that smoking marijuana will likely lead to the use of harder drugs. The man whose story is shown here first started his drug use with marijuana, which led to his abuse of crystal meth (also known as speed or crank).

Students who smoke marijuana get lower grades and are less likely to graduate from high school, compared with their non-smoking peers.[3] Marijuana compromises the ability to learn and remember information. So the more a person smokes marijuana, the more likely he or she is to fall behind in gaining intellectual, job, and social skills.[4] Many users lose athletic endurance as a result of smoking. Young athletes find their performance is not what it could be because the THC in marijuana affects timing, movement, and coordination.

Workers who smoke marijuana have more problems on the job than coworkers who do not smoke. Several studies have linked workers' marijuana use with increased absences, tardiness, accidents, worker's compensation claims, and job turnover.[5]

Depression, anxiety, and personality disturbances are all linked to marijuana use. Marijuana clearly has the potential to cause problems in how a user copes with daily life and even make a person's problems worse.

Symptoms of Marijuana Addiction

Long-term marijuana use can lead to addiction. In 1999, more than 220,000 people entering drug abuse treatment programs reported marijuana was their main drug of abuse.[6] Signs of marijuana addiction include:

- Continuing to use marijuana despite significant problems related to use
- Craving marijuana
- Finding it hard to resist marijuana when it is available
- Cutting back on important social, occupational, or recreational activities because of use
- Unsuccessful attempts to cut down or control use
- Spending a lot of time engaged in activities necessary to obtain marijuana

When to Seek Help and Who Can Help

Some frequent, long-term marijuana users show signs of a lack of motivation called amotivational syndrome.[7] Some symptoms include not caring about what happens in their lives and having no desire to work. Users are tired all the time and ignore how they look, not taking time for grooming. Friend and family relationships may be deteriorating due to the addiction. Depression can also set in and cause more problems for the marijuana abuser.

There is no magic formula to prevent teenage drug use. Still, parents can help by talking with their kids about the dangers of using marijuana and other drugs. Parents need to remain active in their children's lives. Research shows that appropriate parental monitoring can reduce future drug use.[8]

Other places to seek help can be friends, a school counselor, a teacher, a family doctor, or any other adult the user can trust. Drug abuse prevention programs also exist in communities and

PERCENTAGE OF STUDENTS REPORTING MARIJUANA / HASHISH USE, 2003			
FREQUENCY OF USE	PERCENTAGE		
	8th Graders	10th Graders	12th Graders
Daily	1.0%	3.6%	6.0%
30-Day	7.5%	17.0%	21.2%
Annual	12.8%	28.2%	34.9%
Lifetime	17.5%	36.4%	46.1%

Source: Monitoring the Future Study

▲ *Hashish is the resin taken from the top of the hemp plant. Some users prefer to smoke hashish.*

hospitals. Drug treatment centers and drop-in crisis centers are also available for support.

Treatment for Marijuana Abuse

Up until a few years ago, it was hard to find treatment programs specifically for marijuana users. Treatments for marijuana dependence were similar to therapies for other drug abuse problems. These include behavioral therapies, such as cognitive behavioral therapy, multisystemic therapy, individual and group

PERCENT OF STUDENTS REPORTING THAT THEY CURRENTLY USE MARIJUANA, 1999–2003

GRADE	1999	2001	2003
9th	21.7%	19.4%	18.5%
10th	27.8%	24.8%	22.0%
11th	26.7%	25.8%	24.1%
12th	31.5%	26.9%	25.8%
Total	26.7%	23.9%	22.4%

Source: National Survey on Drug Use and Health

counseling, and regular attendance at meetings of support groups like Marijuana Anonymous or Narcotics Anonymous.

There are currently no medications to treat marijuana dependence. However, recent discoveries about the workings of the THC receptors have raised the possibility of eventually developing a medication that will block the intoxicating effects of THC.[9] Such a medication might be used to prevent a relapse to marijuana abuse by lessening or eliminating its appeal.

Drug Prevention

Growing up is not an easy part of human life. Young adults experience sudden body changes, along with mood changes and feelings of insecurity. All teens experience these feelings and emotions. Most teens, however, do not use drugs. Educating yourself with self-help books or online sources about the dangers of drug use can be a good place to start.

Another area to consider in drug prevention is who your peers are. Choose your circle of friends wisely to eliminate any chances of being exposed to drugs or the opportunity to try them. It is

Though it may look like a harmless plant in this photo, the negative aspects of marijuana use are very real. It is wisest to stay away from it and the people who use it.

best to participate in healthy social activities—like sports or school clubs—that will keep you busy. There are many activities to choose from that do not involve drugs. Map out your life goals to help visualize your dreams, and realize that abusing drugs will keep you from achieving them.

adverse—Harmful to one's well-being.

chemotherapy—The use of chemicals to treat diseases or mental illnesses. Commonly used for cancer treatment.

dopamine—A neurotransmitter, or chemical, in the brain that carries messages between the brain cells and regulates physical movement, motivation, emotion, and pleasurable feelings.

drug paraphernalia—Accessory items that people use to carry, conceal, inject, smoke, or sniff drugs.

euphoria—Feeling of joy and good health.

illicit—Illegal.

mainstream—A generally accepted activity or way of thinking.

narcotics—Any drug, regardless of its effects, that is restricted by the government in the same way that addictive pain-relieving drugs are legally limited.

pharmacopeia—A book distributed by a recognized authority that describes chemicals, drugs, and medicinal preparations.

receptor—A specialized protein on the surface of a cell that serves as a binding site for a specific chemical group, molecule, or virus.

resin—Any solid or semisolid natural organic substance that is sticky and normally yellow or brown in color.

synthetic—Not genuine, made by artificial means; man-made.

Chapter Notes

Chapter 1. What Is Marijuana?

1. National Institute on Drug Abuse, "Marijuana Abuse Research Report," January 17, 2003, <http://www.nida.nih.gov/ResearchReports/ Marijuana/Marijuana2.html> (September 8, 2004).

2. Ibid.

3. National Institute on Drug Abuse, "Marijuana: Facts Parents Need to Know," January 17, 2003, <http://www.drugabuse.gov/MarijBroch/ MarijparentsN.html> (September 8, 2004).

4. Ibid.

5. National Institute on Drug Abuse, "Marijuana Abuse Research Report."

6. ———, "Marijuana: Facts Parents Need to Know."

7. Ibid.

8. Ibid.

Chapter 2. History of Marijuana

1. UKCIA, "Industrial Potential of Hemp," n.d., <http://www.ukcia .org/industrial> (September 8, 2004).

2. Ibid.

3. ShirtMagic, "Industrial Hemp Information Page," n.d., <http:// shirtmagic.com/whyhemp.html> (March 25, 2004).

4. "Evidence Supporting Marijuana's Medical Value, *NORML,* 2004, <http://www.norml.org> (September 8, 2004).

5. "Marijuana Use in America Before 1937; Sowing the Seeds for Prohibition," *NORML Report on Sixty Years of Marijuana Prohibition in the U.S.,* March 17, 2002, <www.norml.org/index.cfm?Group_ID=4429> (September 8, 2004).

6. Ibid.

7. Highbeam Research, "History of Marijuana Use," *Columbia Encyclopedia, Sixth Edition,* 2004, <http://www.encyclopedia.com/html/ section/marijuan_HistoryofMarijuanaUse.asp> (September 8, 2004).

8. DrugCulture.com, "Marijuana and the Drug War," *Marijuana Info,* 2003, <http://marijuana.drug-culture.com/marijuana_drug_war.asp> (September 8, 2004).

9. *Frontline,* "A Social History of America's Most Popular Drugs," *Drug Wars,* 2000, <http://www.pbs.org/wgbh/pages/frontline/shows/drugs/buyers/ socialhistory.html> (September 8, 2004).

10. Ibid.

11. Ibid.

12. United Nations Office for Drug Control and Crime Prevention, *Global Illicit Drug Trends 1999* (New York: UNODCCP, 1999), p. 91, as reprinted by Common Sense for Drug Policy, <http://www .drugwarfacts.org/marijuan.htm> (September 8, 2004).

13. Drug Policy Information Clearinghouse, "Marijuana," March 31, 2004, <http://www.whitehousedrugpolicy.gov/publications/factsht/ marijuana/index.html> (September 8, 2004).

14. National Institute on Drug Abuse, "Marijuana: Facts Parents Need to Know," January 17, 2003, <http://www.drugabuse.gov/MarijBroch/ MarijparentsN.html> (September 8, 2004).

15. Highbeam Research, "History of Marijuana Use."

16. Ibid.

17. Ibid.

18. DrugCulture.com, "Marijuana and the Drug War."

19. "Part I," *NORML Report on Sixty Years of Marijuana Prohibition in the U.S.,* March 17, 2002, <www.norml.org/index.cfm?Group_ID=4429> (October 2003).

20. "Summary of Active State Medical Marijuana Programs," *Medical Use,* July 26, 2002, <http://www.norml.org/index.cfm?Group_ID=3391> (September 8, 2004).

21. National Institute on Drug Abuse, "The Science of Medical Marijuana," May 15, 2003, <http://www.nida.nih.gov/drugpages/marijuana .html> (September 8, 2004).

22. Ibid.

Chapter 3. Marijuana's Effects on the Body

1. Narconon of Southern California, "Marijuana in Your System," *Marijuana Detox,* 2003, <http://www.marijuana-detox.com/marijuana-in -system.htm> (September 8, 2004).

2. National Institute on Drug Abuse, "The Science of Medical Marijuana," May 15, 2003, <http://www.nida.nih.gov/drugpages/marijuana .html> (September 8, 2004).

3. Ibid.

4. Narconon Southern California, "Effective Solutions to Drug Addiction & Alcoholism Since 1971," 2001, <http://www.marijuanaaddiction.info/> (September 8, 2004).

5. National Institute on Drug Abuse, "Marijuana Abuse Research Report," May 15, 2003, <http://www.nida.nih.gov/ResearchReports/Marijuana/Marijuana3.html#physicalhealth> (September 8, 2004).

6. Narconon of Southern California, "Marijuana in Your System."

Chapter 4. How Marijuana Is Cultivated and Sold

1. Narconon of Southern California, "Marijuana Prices," 2001, <http://www.marijuanaaddiction.info/marijuana-prices.htm> (September 8, 2004).

2. Lana D. Harrison, Michael Backenheimer, and James A. Inciardi, "Marijuana Supply, Sales and Seizures," *Cedro,* 1996, <http://www.cedro-uva.org/lib/harrison.cannabis.04.html> (September 8, 2004).

3. Highbeam Research, "History of Marijuana Use," *Columbia Encyclopedia, Sixth Edition,* 2004, <http://www.encyclopedia.com/html/section/marijuan_HistoryofMarijuanaUse.asp> (September 8, 2004).

4. Ibid.

5. Ibid.

6. Ibid.

7. Narconon of Southern California, "Marijuana Prices."

8. Ibid.

9. Ibid.

10. Ibid.

11. Ibid.

12. Ibid.

13. "Part I," *NORML Report on Sixty Years of Marijuana Prohibition in the U.S.,* March 17, 2002, <www.norml.org/index.cfm?Group_ID=4429> (September 22, 2004).

14. Ibid.

15. Ibid.

16. Ibid.

17. Ibid.

18. Ibid.

19. Ibid.

20. Federal Bureau of Investigation, *Crime in America: FBI Uniform Crime Reports 2002* (Washington, D.C.: U.S. Government Printing Office, 2003), p. 234, as reprinted by Common Sense for Drug Policy, <http://www.drugwarfacts.org/marijuan.htm> (September 8, 2004).

21. Ibid.

Chapter 5. Avoiding Marijuana and Getting Help

1. The Associated Press, "Teens: Pot Easier to Buy than Beer," *CBSNews.com,* August 20, 2002, <http://www.cbsnews.com/stories/2002/08/20/health/printable519228.shtml> (February 27, 2004).

2. Ibid.

3. National Institute on Drug Abuse, "The Science of Medical Marijuana," May 15, 2003, <http://www.nida.nih.gov/drugpages/marijuana.html> (September 8, 2004).

4. Ibid.

5. Ibid.

6. National Institute on Drug Abuse, "How Does Marijuana Affect School, Work, and Social Life," January 22, 2003, <http://www.drugabuse.gov/ResearchReports/ Marijuana/Marijuana5.html> (September 8, 2004).

7. National Institute on Drug Abuse, "Marijuana: Facts Parents Need to Know," January 17, 2003, <http://www.drugabuse.gov/MarijBroch/MarijparentsN.html> (September 8, 2004).

8. Ibid.

9. National Institute on Drug Abuse, "Marijuana," July 14, 2004, <http://www.nida.nih.gov/Infofax/marijuana.html> (September 8, 2004).

Further Reading

Barbour, Scott, ed. *Drug Legalization.* San Diego, Calif.: Greenhaven Press, 2000.

Bellenir, Karen, ed. *Drug Information for Teens: Health Tips About the Physical and Mental Effects of Substance Abuse.* Detroit: Omnigraphics, 2002.

Connolly, Sean. *Marijuana.* Chicago: Heinemann Library, 2003.

Dorsman, Jerry. *How to Quit Drugs for Good: A Complete Self-Help Guide.* Roseville, Calif.: Prima Publishing, 1998.

Earleywine, Mitchell. *Understanding Marijuana: A New Look at the Scientific Evidence.* New York: Oxford University Press, 2002.

Gerdes, Louise I., ed. *Marijuana.* San Diego, Calif.: Greenhaven Press, 2002.

Hasday, Judy L. and Therese De Angelis. *Marijuana.* Philadelphia: Chelsea House, 2000.

Iversen, Leslie. *The Science of Marijuana.* New York: Oxford University Press, 2000.

Narcotics Anonymous, Basic Text, 20th Anniversary Edition. Van Nuys, Calif.: NA, 2003.

Schaler, Jeffrey, Ph.D. *Addiction Is a Choice.* Peru, Ill.: Carus Publishing, 2000.

Schleichert, Elizabeth. *Marijuana.* Berkeley Heights, N.J.: Enslow Publishers, Inc., 2001.

Somdahl, Gary L. *Marijuana Drug Dangers.* Berkeley Heights, N.J.: Enslow Publishers, Inc., 2000.

Stanley, Debbie. *Marijuana and Your Lungs: The Incredibly Disgusting Story.* New York: Rosen Central, 2000.

Williams, Mary E. *Marijuana.* Farmington Hills, Mich.: Gale Group, 2003.

Phone Numbers to Call for Help

Marijuana Anonymous
1–800–766–6779

NAADAC, The Association for Addiction Professionals
1–800–548–0497

Narcotics Anonymous
1–818–773–9999

National Drug Information Treatment and Referral
1–800–662–HELP